Creature of the Night

Straining to make his voice seem normal, he said, "Yes, Mother, it's me. I was just going to bed. Good night."

He put a paw to his throat in horror. He sounded as if he had been gargling with razor blades.

"Are you all right, Russell? You sound a little hoarse."

"I'm fine! Just got a little frog in my throat!"

Actually, it sounded more like he had a Gila monster in there.

"All right," called his mother. "But if it's not gone in the morning, I'm taking your temperature, and no arguments!"

"Yes . . . *Mother.*"

Well, that was over. Now what?

The directions! he thought again. *I've got to look at those directions!*

Moving cautiously, Russell continued to his room. But the waxing moon, just past the halfway mark, was shining through his window. It caught his eye and he gasped. He felt as if it were tied to his heart by a silver thread.

He crossed to the sill, raised the window, and leaned out.

The moon was *calling* him.

And deep within his monsterish breast something stirred in answer—something that insisted he could stay inside no longer. . . .

THE MAGIC SHOP BOOKS
by Bruce Coville

The Monster's Ring
Russell Crannaker, bullied all his life,
gets a chance to fight back when he is given
a monstrous magical item.

Jeremy Thatcher, Dragon Hatcher
Jeremy Thatcher's deepest desires take flight
when he is forced to raise a demanding
dragon hatchling.

Jennifer Murdley's Toad
Jennifer Murdley, a girl "in a plain brown wrapper,"
buys a talking toad who knows a thing or two about
the true nature of beauty.

The Skull of Truth
Charlie Eggleston, who can't help lying,
suddenly must tell the truth and nothing *but* when
he takes the Skull from Mr. Elives' shop.

Juliet Dove, Queen of Love
Shy Juliet Dove suddenly becomes the most
popular girl in school when she wears the ancient
amulet given to her at the magic shop.

OTHER BOOKS BY BRUCE COVILLE

Odds Are Good:
An *Oddly Enough* and *Odder Than Ever* Omnibus

Thor's Wedding Day

The Unicorn Treasury:
Stories, Poems, and Unicorn Lore

The Prince of Butterflies

The Monsters of Morley Manor

Armageddon Summer (with Jane Yolen)

The Monster's Ring

❖

The Monster's Ring

A MAGIC SHOP BOOK

Bruce Coville

ILLUSTRATED BY
KATHERINE COVILLE

MAGIC CARPET BOOKS
HARCOURT, INC.
ORLANDO AUSTIN NEW YORK SAN DIEGO LONDON

www.HarcourtBooks.com

First published 1982
First Magic Carpet Books edition 2008

Magic Carpet Books is a trademark of Harcourt, Inc.,
registered in the United States of America and/or other jurisdictions.

The Library of Congress has cataloged the hardcover edition as follows:
Coville, Bruce.
The monster's ring/by Bruce Coville.
p. cm.
"A Magic Shop Book."
Summary: A timid boy, eager to frighten the school bully
on Halloween night, acquires a magic ring and the power
to change himself into a hideous monster.
[1. Monsters—Fiction.   2. Bullies—Fiction.   3. Halloween—Fiction.
4. Schools—Fiction.   5. Magic—Fiction.]   I. Title.
PZ7.C8344Mo   2002
[Fic]—dc21   2002003537
ISBN 978-0-15-204618-7
ISBN 978-0-15-206442-6 pb

Text set in New Baskerville

A C E G H F D B

Printed in the United States of America

This is still *for Orion*

Contents

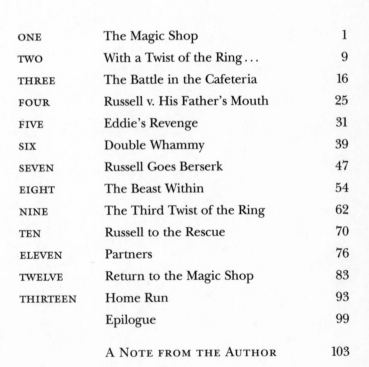

The Monster's Ring

ONE

✤

The Magic Shop

Russell Crannaker glanced up and down the alley. He was alone.

Perfect. He could practice in peace.

Putting up his arms, Russell staggered forward. He rolled back his eyes so only the whites were showing. Then he began to moan.

Fantastic! He was going to be great as Frankenstein's monster—the best ever.

Russell relaxed and grinned. Halloween should be all right this year after all.

He moaned and lurched forward again.

Frankenstein. Boy, would he love to actually *be* Frankenstein's monster for a while. Then he'd show that Eddie a thing or two. He could see it now: Eddie kneeling in front of him, whining, begging, pleading for mercy.

He could even hear Eddie's voice: "Please, Russell. Please don't hurt me. Please. *Please!*"

Russell smiled. It was a pleasant daydream. But his smile quickly turned to a frown.

Something was wrong.

Eddie was still talking!

"Oh, no! Save me, save me! It's the horrible Crankenstein! Hey, Crannaker, what's up? You lose your marbles?"

Russell opened his eyes and turned pale. Eddie, six inches taller than Russell and made mostly of mouth and muscle, was standing at the end of the alley. "Come here, twink," he sneered. "I'll make you *really* look like Frankenstein."

Russell started to shake. So far that day, Eddie had poked him, punched him, called him names, and smashed him in the face with a cream-filled cupcake. Under the circumstances, only one thing made sense.

Russell did it.

He ran.

"Hey, Crannaker!" bellowed Eddie. "Whassa matter? You afraid?"

Afraid? Of course he was afraid! These days he lived in fear of what Eddie might do next.

He rounded the back corner of the alley and tripped over a row of garbage cans. One fell, spreading trash from wall to wall. Eddie, racing around the corner after him, struck something slimy and slid to his seat. "I'll get you for this, Crannaker!" he roared.

I've got to get out of here, Russell thought desperately. *Got to get away . . . now!*

He was off like a shot, barreling down some back street. Without thinking, without looking, he turned another corner, and then another.

Suddenly everything was quiet.

Russell stopped. Where was Eddie?

He looked around.

To his surprise, he was alone. Not only that, he was on a street that was completely new to him. That bothered him a little, but it was no real problem. He knew Kennituck Falls fairly well. He couldn't be far from a main street.

He walked to the next corner, figuring that would take him back to where he had started.

It didn't.

He turned right again—and then again. He was confused now. And scared. Not scared the way he had been when Eddie was after him. He was scared because *Kennituck Falls was too small to get lost in. . . .*

It was starting to get dark. A fog began to rise, the mist curling around his feet like snakes made out of smoke.

Russell stopped again. He had reached a dead-end street. It was lined with shops he had never seen before. They were closed—all except one. Directly ahead of him, a light burning in its window, crouched a store that took his breath away. The sign in the curved window, written in old-fashioned letters, read:

ELIVES' MAGIC SUPPLIES
S. H. ELIVES, PROP.

3

Russell felt a surge of delight. He was crazy about magic anyhow. But in October, when it seemed as if anything could happen, he was consumed with a desire to experience it. His worries about being lost disappeared. He *had* to see what was in that shop!

He hurried forward. Through a window dark with the grime of years, he could see a crammed display of typical magician's stock: big decks of cards, top hats, Chinese rings, silk scarves. But there was more here— dark boxes with mysterious designs, capes with dragons on them, a skull with a candle on its top. . . .

He loved it.

Glancing over his shoulder to make sure his enemy was nowhere in sight, he opened the door.

A small bell tinkled overhead as Russell stepped in. He looked around uncertainly. A sweet, mysterious aroma filled the air, but the shop was empty. Not only were there no other customers, there was not even a clerk in sight.

He didn't care; he was too thrilled by the contents of the place, which was jam-packed from top to bottom with magic equipment. The wall to his right held a section of live animals—doves and rabbits, mostly, for pulling out of hats, but also lizards, toads, and snakes.

I wonder what they're *for,* thought Russell.

Then his attention was attracted by a stack of books—old, leather-bound volumes with thick ridges on their spines. The top book on the pile was titled *Mystery and Illusion.* Beneath it was *A Traveler's Guide to Other Worlds.*

Just past the books, resting on a pair of dark red

sawhorses, was a large box for the old trick of sawing someone in half.

Beyond the box, stretching across the back of the shop, was a long wooden counter with a dragon painted on its side.

On top of the counter sat an old-fashioned brass cash register.

On top of the cash register sat a stuffed owl.

At least, Russell thought the owl was stuffed—until it swiveled its head toward him. It blinked its brown-flower eyes, then uttered a low hoot.

From beyond the curtain that covered the door behind the counter came a voice that made Russell think of dead leaves scraping along the sidewalk in the October wind.

"Peace, Uwila. I know he's there."

A wrinkled hand pulled the curtain aside.

Out shuffled an old man.

Old? *Ancient* was more like it. His withered brown skin reminded Russell of dried mushrooms. He was shorter than Russell, and probably weighed less. Yet for some reason—maybe the eyes that glittered like black diamonds below his bristling brow—he seemed very, very strong. He walked around the counter and came to stand in front of Russell.

"Why are you here?"

Russell shivered. "I...I just came in to look around."

The old man shook his head. "Young man, no one comes in *my* shop just to 'look around.' Get to the point. What do you need?"

"Honestly, sir—I just came in to see what you have."

The old man arched one eyebrow and squinted his other eye shut. "Well, you've seen it. Now—*what do you need?*"

The tone of his voice made it clear to Russell that he had better need something.

He glanced around desperately.

"I don't even see any prices."

"How much money do you have?" asked the old man.

Fishing in his pocket, Russell found a crumpled dollar bill—lunch money he had saved by being too nervous to eat. "Just this. But I don't think—"

"That will be fine!" snapped the old man, snatching it away from him. "Stand still."

Russell looked at him in surprise.

"Quiet!" said the old man, though Russell had not spoken a word.

Russell stood as if frozen.

The old man stared at him, then closed his eyes and bent his head, almost as if he were listening to something. After a moment, he opened his eyes and said, "Wait here." Then he turned and disappeared back through the curtain.

Russell felt as if his feet had frozen to the floor; he couldn't have moved if he had tried.

After what seemed like hours, the old man reappeared, carrying a small box. "Here," he said, extending the box to Russell. "Take this. It's...what you came here to get."

Russell's fingers trembled as he held out his hand to accept the package.

The old man leaned even closer. Staring directly into Russell's eyes, speaking in a low hiss that made the boy feel as if a cold wind were running down his spine, he said, "For Ishtar's sake—*be careful!*"

Then he dropped the box into Russell's waiting fingers.

Russell looked around wildly. Through the front window he could see that it had gotten very dark outside.

"Take the side door," said the old man, gesturing to his right. "It will get you home more...quickly."

He began to laugh.

Russell spotted the small door at the side of the shop and bolted for it. To his astonishment, he found himself back in the alley where he had started.

For a moment, Russell thought he must have had some strange daydream, or even a hallucination.

Then he realized that he was clutching something in his hand.

Slowly, nervously, he opened his fingers.

✦

TWO

With a Twist of the Ring...

He was holding a small box.

Across the top, in flaming red letters, were the words:

THE MONSTER'S RING

Russell smiled. He was very fond of monsters. (In fact, he had the largest collection of monster magazines of anyone in the fifth grade.)

Using his fingernail, he slit the tape that held the box shut.

Inside was a ring made of cheap metal. Set in its top was a green stone carved in the shape of a monster's face.

Delighted, Russell took out the ring and slipped it onto his finger. As he did, a sudden chill ran through his body.

He shook his head and shivered.

In the bottom of the box lay a neatly folded piece

of paper. Curious, Russell lifted it out. The paper was old and yellowed, and it crinkled as he unfolded it.

At the top of the paper was a picture of a monster—the same monster as on the ring. Its arms were spread across the page as if holding everything written beneath it.

Directly below the monster's chin, in big letters, were the words HOW TO WORK THE MONSTER'S RING.

Work it? thought Russell. *How could you "work" a ring?*

It must mean how to *wear* it.

But who needed instructions to wear a ring?

He read on.

"To change yourself into a hideous monster, place the ring on the ring finger of your right hand. Grasp it with your left hand. Turn the ring to the left as you repeat this chant..."

Russell shook his head in disgust. "To change yourself into a hideous monster!" He had sworn off that kind of garbage after he wasted all that money on those useless "X-Ray Specs" he bought from the back of a *Muck Critter* comic.

He crumpled the paper, crammed it into his pocket, and headed for home.

His mother was waiting for him at the door.

"Where have you been, Russell?" she asked.

He could hear the worry in her voice: It was always there, no matter what time he got home.

"Out," he said with a shrug.

"Well, what have you been doing?"

He shrugged again. "Nothing."

Mrs. Crannaker sighed. "Well, supper is ready, and you're not. Go get cleaned up. Go on . . . hurry . . . hurry *up,* Russell. *Hurry!*"

Supper was a typical Crannaker family meal. His mother fussed over him as he ate. (She fussed over him a lot.) His father talked on and on (and *on!*) about some problem he was having at work. And Russell, who had no appetite, sat chasing peas around mashed-potato mountains with his fork.

He was considering telling his parents about the problems he was having with Eddie. But his father had moved on to one of his pet theories—something about the future of civilization—and he wouldn't wind down for hours.

Russell loved his father, but trying to get a word in edgewise when he was talking was like trying to stop a freight train by standing in front of it: Either way, you were bound to get run down. So Russell simply tuned out.

Fortunately, Mr. Crannaker didn't seem to care if anyone actually listened to him. As long as he was talking, he was happy. Russell often heard him at night, chattering away over some work he had brought home from the office. He carried on a running dialogue with the television set, and even argued back to the newspaper while he was reading it.

The night wore on. Russell did his homework, then read some of a very spooky book called *The House with a Clock in Its Walls*. He had almost forgotten about the ring until it caught on his shirt as he was undressing for bed. He grinned. The monster on top really was neat.

Oh, why not? he thought. *No one will know if I make a fool of myself here in my own room.*

He took out the directions and spread them on his dresser top. Then he gave the ring a twist—one only—as he whispered the chant from the top of the page:

"Powers Dark and Powers Bright,
I call you now, as is my right.
Unleash the magic of this ring,
And change me to a monstrous thing!"

He waited, feeling very silly.

Nothing happened.

"X-Ray Specs," he said, and shrugged. He headed for the bathroom to wash up, more disappointed than he cared to admit.

Halfway down the hall, Russell felt a strange sensation in his forehead, almost as if something was trying to break through the skin. It didn't hurt. It was just...weird. He put his hand on his brow and felt something sharp and hard. He tried to pull it off. No luck.

He ran to the bathroom, looked in the mirror, and nearly fainted.

He had horns coming out of his forehead—horns an inch long, and getting longer!

Mouth agape, Russell watched the transformation. Suddenly hair began to sprout from his face. He needed a shave.

Shave? He needed a lawn mower!

He touched the horns. They seemed to have stopped growing. Mottled brown and yellow, they were almost three inches long and ended in gleaming points, wickedly sharp.

Beneath the horns his brows met in a single shaggy line that ran straight across his forehead. Beneath that line flashed two yellow eyes, holding a strange hint of inner fire. His nose—flatter than an old prizefighter's—was nearly lost in the thick beard that hid his neck and chin.

The backs of his hands were covered with curling black fur. He wanted to scream. No—that would only bring his parents.

Suddenly he realized that even though he was frightened, he was also excited. Strange as it was, this was the most *interesting* thing that had ever happened to him.

He looked in the mirror and snarled.

The sight—and sound—made him jump.

He tried it again.

"Boy, would that ever do a number on Eddie."

He chuckled at the idea, sounding like an angry bear.

This was ridiculous. He must be dreaming.

He pinched himself to prove it.

Unfortunately, his fingernails were now deadly claws. He drew blood, and the sharp pain convinced him that he was, indeed, awake.

13

Panic set in.

How long would this last? What if he couldn't turn back?

The idea caught in his mind and scared him witless. What would his mother say? What *wouldn't* his father say? This would give his dad material for hours of passionate, rambling speeches concerning the woeful tale of the thoughtless son who messed about with magic and was turned into a hairy monster as punishment.

Wait a minute. He hadn't finished reading the directions. Maybe they explained how to turn back.

Opening the bathroom door he peered out cautiously.

Good. His parents were still downstairs.

He stepped out and headed for his room. But as a monster, he did not have as much self-control as when he was a kid. Without intending to, he began to stomp down the hall.

"Russell!" cried a voice from below. "Is that *you?*"

It was his mother.

He froze.

"Russell?"

He had to answer her; if he didn't, she would come up to see what was going on. Straining to make his voice seem normal, he said, "Yes, Mother, it's me. I was just going to bed. Good night."

He put a paw to his throat in horror. He sounded as if he had been gargling with razor blades.

"Are you all right, Russell? You sound a little hoarse."

"I'm fine! Just got a little frog in my throat!"

Actually, it sounded more like he had a Gila monster in there.

"All right," called his mother. "But if it's not gone in the morning, I'm taking your temperature, and no arguments!"

"Yes... *Mother.*"

Well, that was over. Now what?

The directions! he thought again. *I've got to look at those directions!*

Moving more cautiously now, Russell continued to his room. But the waxing moon, just past the halfway mark, was shining through his window. It caught his eye and he gasped. He felt as if it were tied to his heart by a silver thread.

He crossed to the sill, raised the window, and leaned out.

The moon was *calling* him.

And deep within his monsterish breast something stirred in answer—something that insisted he could stay inside no longer.

Filled with longing, Russell gazed out at the night, all black and silver and magic. It was a good fifteen feet to the ground, but somehow that didn't seem to matter. Suddenly he vaulted over and out.

He landed in a crouch.

Sniffing the air, he glanced around—then ran howling into the darkness.

✥

THREE

The Battle
in the Cafeteria

Russell bounded joyfully out of bed. What a fantastic dream!

Suddenly he stopped dead in his tracks.

There were hairy feet sticking out of his pajamas.

He sat down.

Slowly.

So it wasn't a dream.

He shook his head as images began to flicker through his mind. He saw himself—his monster self—in action: growling at late shoppers, swinging on street lamps, and—his cheeks burned at the memory—chasing cars down Main Street.

On all fours.

Snapping at the hubcaps!

Cripes. This was embarrassing.

He groaned as he remembered what had come next. Even now he wasn't sure how he had escaped from all those policemen.

It was a good thing his monster legs could move so fast.

He shuddered.

So he had made it back to his room somehow.

Wonderful.

Now what?

"Russell! Time for breakfast!"

His mother's voice doubled his panic, and he almost howled in despair.

He slapped a paw across his hairy face. Howling was the last thing he ought to do at this point. But how could he go down there like this? What could he possibly say? "Morning, Mom. Morning, Dad. What's wrong? Oh, *this*. Yes, it is a little weird, isn't it? . . ."

No, that would never do.

He stood up to pace the room and spotted a paper on his dresser.

The directions! What a dope! How could he have forgotten them? Being a monster must have addled his brains.

He snatched up the paper.

There it was, in black and white: the way to turn back.

He sighed. His mother had told him time and again, "Read *all* the directions before you start a project."

Score one for Mom.

He examined the paper carefully, this time reading every word.

HOW TO WORK THE MONSTER'S RING

To change yourself into a hideous monster, place the ring on the ring finger of your right hand. Grasp it with your left hand. Turn the ring to the left as you repeat this chant:

> Powers Dark and Powers Bright,
> I call you now, as is my right.
> Unleash the magic of this ring,
> And change me to a monstrous thing!

The strength of the spell depends on how many twists you give the ring:

> Twist it once, you're horned and haired;
> Twist it twice and fangs are bared;
> Twist it thrice? No one has dared!

Use with caution, *and never on the night of a full moon.* To return to normal, turn the ring to the right, repeating this chant:

> Powers Bright and Powers Dark,
> Hark to one who bears your mark.
> Let now my shape return to me,
> And make me as I used to be!

HAVE FUN!

Trembling, Russell took the ring in his claws and twisted it as he repeated the final verse.

It worked! He could feel his horns beginning to shrink, his hair growing shorter, his claws turning back into nails.

He wanted to shout for joy.

Then something occurred to him—a thought his panic had blinded him to before. If he had an antidote, *he could become a monster anytime he wanted.*

For the first time in his life, the future looked beautiful.

Russell was sitting in the cafeteria. School had been fun so far. The place was buzzing with rumors about the "maniac" who had run amok in town last night, and it was all Russell could do to keep a straight face.

Missy Freebaker sat down next to him. "Did you hear about the monster, Russell?" she asked excitedly. "Isn't it scary?"

"I think it's silly. There's no such thing as monsters."

"Well, how come so many people saw this one?"

"Maybe they were hallucinating."

Missy scowled. Russell smiled and turned to his lunch.

Then Eddie sat down opposite him.

Russell groaned as he felt a familiar lump form in his stomach. There was no doubt that Eddie would do something rotten. So there was no sense in even trying to eat. It wasn't worth the effort.

He looked up. Eddie was grinning at him, with all his teeth showing. Russell knew that grin well. It was a very bad sign.

A sudden crash from the other side of the cafeteria caused Russell to turn and look.

When he turned back, Eddie was pouring chocolate milk all over his lunch.

Russell got angry. Then he got scared because he was angry. Then the anger became more important again.

He picked up his spoon and smacked Eddie's hand.

"What do you think you're doing, Crannaker?" screamed Eddie. He shoved Russell's tray so that it smashed into his chest.

Without thinking, Russell took what was left of his milk and threw it at Eddie. The carton struck his chest, and chocolate milk erupted out of it, spattering all over Eddie's face.

Eddie howled in rage. Lunging across the table, he grabbed Russell's shirt, shouting about how Russell was going to be sorry he'd been born, and how they were going to need a spatula to get him off the cafeteria walls.

Russell was crying. But he was also smacking Eddie on the head with his spoon, shouting, "Stop it, stip ot, stoop it!"

Eddie didn't stop.

Russell picked up his plate and dumped it on Eddie's head.

Spaghetti flew in all directions.

Eddie screeched. Strings of spaghetti dangled over his ears like some strange new hairdo.

Suddenly Russell realized what he had just done. Eddie had never heard of forgive and forget. He would be after Russell for the rest of his life now. He would wait around every corner, hide behind every bush, ready to jump out and pay Russell back a thousand times for this one insult.

The horror movie of revenge unreeling in Russell's mind was stopped short by someone grabbing his shoulder. He was wrenched around to find himself face-to-face with his teacher, Miss Snergal.

"What is going on here?" she cried. She was so angry she could hardly get the words out.

Russell and Eddie both started talking.

"Be quiet!" she snapped. She marched them both out of the cafeteria. "You go wash up," she said to Eddie. "Russell, you wait here until I come for you. After lunch we'll make a little trip to the principal's office." She stood him beside the door and disappeared back into the cafeteria.

Russell slid to the floor. *The principal!* Old Man Rafschnitz was the most feared person at Boardman Road Elementary. Kids turned white at the very mention of his name. And now he, Russell, had broken the rules.

He was being sent to *that* office.

He would have to face . . . "The Beast of Boardman Road."

What had made him do all that, anyway? Usually

he just took Eddie's abuse without saying or doing anything, and ended up feeling rotten as a result.

To Russell's surprise, he realized that he did not feel rotten now. In fact, if you didn't count his fear of Mr. Rafschnitz, he felt pretty good.

Just then Eddie came swaggering back from the bathroom. He still had spaghetti sauce in his ears, but he was smirking as if he owned the world. He had been through this a thousand times, after all. In fact, Eddie spent so much time in Mr. Rafschnitz's office that most kids thought he must have a special chair set aside just for him. Some even claimed it had his name on it.

Leaning against the door, Eddie smiled down at Russell and said fiendishly, "Wait till school's over, Crannaker. I'm gonna mop the hallways with your face."

Russell began to tremble. Clasping his hands together to keep them from shaking, he felt the ring.

The ring!

A smile flickered over his face.

"Try it, bozo. See what happens."

The look on Eddie's face was perfect. He couldn't believe Russell would dare talk to him like that.

Russell began to chuckle. He couldn't believe it, either. He, Russell, the meek and mild, was making tough Eddie squirm.

He laughed out loud. As he did, Miss Snergal stepped back out of the cafeteria. "I don't see what's so funny, Mr. Crannaker," she snapped. "I had hoped that by now you would have realized the seriousness of what you've done."

"Oh, yes, ma'am," said Russell. He scrambled to his feet, meek and mild again. "I do. Oh, do I ever!"

"Good. You can explain *that* to Mr. Rafschnitz."

✦

Russell v. His Father's Mouth

Mr. Rafschnitz's face was beet red, and his nostrils flared out like a horse's. Just the sight of him was enough to turn Russell into jelly. He had a horrible feeling that he was going to melt and slide right off his chair.

"Well," growled Mr. Rafschnitz, "what do you have to say for yourself?"

Russell tried to think of an answer. Before he could come up with one, Mr. Rafschnitz began to pound his desk so hard that all the drawers in the filing cabinet rattled.

"Never mind the excuses! I hear excuses all day long. What I want to know is what we're going to do about this. Well, I'll *tell* you what we're going to do, Crannaker. We're going to keep an eye on you. We're going to watch every move you make. One false step—*one teeny-tiny move in the wrong direction*—and YOU'VE HAD IT!"

The roaring was giving Russell a headache. He

looked down at the floor and nearly choked on the boulder growing in his stomach.

"I'm pleased to see you're properly ashamed," gloated Mr. Rafschnitz. "I have called your father. He'll be picking you up after school. He will, I'm sure, have much to say to you."

The boulder pushed Russell's stomach down to the bottom of his shoes and squashed it.

Mr. Rafschnitz was right. Russell's father had plenty to say to him. And he had been saying it from the moment Russell got into the car.

Now Russell was having a frightening thought. He was thinking he might try to make his father listen to him. It seemed impossible. But his father had been babbling on for ten minutes already, and Russell thought he was going to explode. He felt as if he had swallowed a stick of dynamite and his father's words were like matches, dropping near the fuse.

"I know life can be tough," Mr. Crannaker was saying. "But violence isn't the answer. You know that, Russell. It shows you to have a small mind, a petty mind, a mind given to a self-centered view of the universe. A mind—"

Russell decided to try it. "But, Dad—"

"This kind of behavior is not what your mother and I expect from you." The flow of words rushed over him like a steamroller. His father wasn't even aware he had *tried* to say anything.

"Dad—"

"You've been raised to know that dumping

spaghetti on people's heads is no way to communicate. And besides—"

"Dad—"

His father barreled on, unaware that Russell had even tried to speak.

The fuse was lit.

"Now, the next time this kid Eddie gives you trouble, I want you to—"

"Dad—"

"—inform the teacher—"

The fuse was burning faster.

"Dad—"

"—her duty to see that—"

The explosion was getting nearer.

"Dad?"

"—students are protected—"

"Dad!"

"—from situations like—"

KA-BOOM!

"DAD, WILL YOU BE QUIET FOR ONCE AND LISTEN TO WHAT I HAVE TO SAY?"

Mr. Crannaker blinked and lapsed into a stunned silence. Russell's cheeks turned red. He couldn't believe what he had just done. He felt like getting out of the car and running. But he couldn't. This might be the only time in his life that his father would be speechless.

"Dad, listen. The teachers can't help. The only time Eddie and I are together is in the cafeteria and on the playground, when there's hundreds of kids around. Even if a teacher is watching, Eddie just punches me anyway and gets in trouble for the fun of it. He doesn't care what happens to him. He doesn't care what happens to anybody. I've been trying to tell you that but you won't listen. You never listen. You're always too busy talking. *And it's driving me crazy!*"

His father stared straight ahead and drove without speaking.

Russell waited until he couldn't stand it any longer. "Well, say something!" he cried.

His father blinked. "I didn't know you felt that way. I thought I was helping you ... offering you guidance ... showing you better ways to live. I always thought I listened to your problems. I've tried to be a good father, Russell. Goodness knows, it's hard enough these days—"

"Dad."

His father blushed. "I'm doing it again, aren't I?" he said softly.

"It's all right," said Russell. "I suppose it's a habit by now."

"But it's a habit I'm going to break," said Mr. Crannaker firmly. "It's about time we had a little two-way communication around here. I shouldn't be the only one to do the talking. I should let you share your thoughts, your dreams, your ideas, your—"

"Dad!"

Mr. Crannaker stopped again. He bit his lip, looking embarrassed.

"Let's not say anything for a while, okay?" said Russell.

Mr. Crannaker paused. "You mean, like practicing?"

"Yeah."

"Okay."

They rode for several minutes in silence, something Russell could not remember having experienced before.

"Listen, Russell," said Mr. Crannaker at last. "About this Eddie thing. I really don't know what to say to help you. Maybe that's why I said so much. But I'll think about it. And I want you to come to talk to me if you have more problems with him. Next time I'll listen. Scout's honor."

Russell smiled. "Thanks." He waited a second, then said, "What about Mom? What is she going to say about this?"

"Truth is, I haven't mentioned it to her yet," said Mr. Crannaker. He stopped for a red light. Turning to Russell, he said, "Why don't we just keep this one between us men?"

Then he gave him a wink.

Russell felt a wave of gratitude.

The light turned green. As they started to roll again, Mr. Crannaker said, "I guess I really haven't listened to much of anything you might have to say lately, Russell. Let's try to catch up some." He paused to think. "Oh, I know: Halloween's this Saturday! Are you going to dress up this year?"

Russell sighed. "I'm not sure. I *was* going to. But some of the kids are saying that's baby stuff."

Mr. Crannaker sighed. "The tragedy of premature maturity. It's a soul killer. Aren't *any* of them dressing up?"

"Well, Jack is working on an alien costume that should be pretty neat."

"That's good," said Mr. Crannaker. "Jack always did act as if he came from another planet."

Russell chuckled. "And Sam is going to be a fat lady."

Mr. Crannaker made a face. "That's not very politically correct. He's apt to have the FLS after him."

"The FLS?"

"The Fat Liberation Society."

Russell laughed out loud. "That's nothing! Wait till you hear what Jimmy Riblin's planning."

"I hesitate to ask," said Mr. Crannaker, who had always claimed that Jimmy was the weirdest kid in Russell's class.

"He's going to put mayonnaise in his mouth and pretend he's a pimple!"

Russell puffed out his cheeks, then poked them with his fingers in a popping gesture to demonstrate.

"Yuck!" cried Mr. Crannaker. He paused, then said, "But what about you? You're so interested in monsters, I would think you would want to dress up like one."

Russell started to describe his plans for a Frankenstein costume, then stopped short as he suddenly realized the incredible truth.

He didn't need a costume.

He had his ring!

✦

FIVE

Eddie's Revenge

"Now, class, if a vampire has three quarts on deposit at the blood bank, and he takes out a pint and a half, how many cups are left?"

Russell smiled. For a fifth-grade teacher, Miss Snergal wasn't bad.

In fact, the whole week had been all right, considering how it had started. Sure, Henry "The Beast" Rafschnitz had been keeping a close eye on him. But Russell had been his usual quiet self ever since the cafeteria incident, so that was no problem. And he had actually gotten the feeling from Miss Snergal that she was pleased he had stood up to Eddie.

As for Eddie himself, he seemed to be avoiding Russell. Had he been put off by the tough talk outside the cafeteria doors? Whatever the reason, Russell enjoyed the freedom from fear, while it lasted.

But the best thing about the week was that Halloween was so close. With its delicious spookiness, the sense of magic in the air, All Hallows' Eve was Russell's favorite holiday, better even than Christmas.

Of course, its arrival meant he did have to deal with his mother's usual reaction to anything involving lots of sweets. ("Eat all that sugar, Russell, and you'll have so many holes in your mouth you could pump air through it and play 'Hail, Columbia' on your teeth!") But he was used to that. Besides, for him, Halloween wasn't candy. It was mystery. Mystery, and a strange tingle, and dreams of ghosts and witches.

And—this year—a perfect opportunity to use his ring.

Friday, the day of the class party, arrived at last. In the morning, Russell carefully packed a grocery sack with some old clothes he had snatched from the rag-bag. Then he put his books on top of them so nobody would see his "costume." Finally, he slipped the ring into his pocket and glanced over the instruction sheet to make sure he had the chants firmly in mind. Then he hurried downstairs and slipped into his spot at the breakfast table.

"What's that, Russell?" asked his mother, pointing at the bag.

"Just some stuff," he said with a shrug.

She pursed her lips. "So you're going to wear a costume?"

Sherlock Mother strikes again, thought Russell.

"Now, Marge," said his father. "I wore a costume when I was in fifth grade. Halloween was a big thing for us. I'm glad Russ is going to dress up. There's a lot to be said for Halloween. Good for the imagination.

Encourages kids to let their minds wander in fresh fields for a while. It even makes *me* stop to think. Didn't you ever wonder what else might be in this world we live in? What hidden marvels we might be missing? Do we know all there is to know? I hardly think so."

Russell listened in astonishment as Mr. Crannaker rambled on. He could not remember the last time his father had actually contradicted his mother. Usually they just talked about completely different things.

Finishing his breakfast, he pushed himself away from the table. His mother started to say something but was overwhelmed by the flow of his father's words.

Russell paused at the door and glanced back at the table. His father, still talking, winked at him. Suddenly Russell understood what was happening: His father was making this entire speech just to keep his mother off his back! He wanted to run to him and hug him. He started back toward the table, but his father made a little gesture with his hand, indicating that Russell should get while the getting was good.

A minute later he was on his bike, heading for school and feeling wonderful. This was going to be the greatest Halloween party of his life.

"Going someplace, Crannaker?"

Russell looked up, and his pleasant dreams came crashing down around him.

Eddie was standing in front of him. His bike was drawn across the sidewalk, blocking Russell's path.

Russell looked around for help. There was none in sight—no one to stop Eddie from turning him into a pulp.

Eddie grinned. "I owe you one, Crannaker."

He let his bike fall and took a step toward Russell.

Russell fumbled for the ring. He pulled it from his pocket, started to put it on.

Whack! Eddie knocked the ring from his hand.

"Hey!" cried Russell, diving for it.

"Come here, twerp," yelled Eddie. He leaped after Russell. Just as Russell reached the ring, Eddie landed on top of him with a crashing thump. Russell's fingers knocked against the ring. It skittered over the curb and into the gutter.

"Get off me, you rotten bully!" screamed Russell.

Eddie laughed. "So you're not as tough as you thought, huh, Crannaker?"

Then he mashed Russell's face into the grass.

"Leave me alone!" cried Russell. But all that came out was "Leemealun!"

Frustrated, he began to kick wildly. He felt his right foot connect with Eddie's back.

"Oh, you wanna get rough, huh?" screamed Eddie. He smashed Russell a good one, knocking the breath completely out of him.

Then he climbed off.

"Remember that the next time you're thinking of calling *me* a bozo, Crannaker."

Wiping his hands in satisfaction, Eddie hopped on his bike and rode off.

Russell rolled over and sat up. Eddie was gone, and the golden morning with him. All that remained was a burning sense of humiliation, and a fierce anger that raged in Russell's heart. He beat his fists against the ground. He wanted to go after Eddie, drag him off that bike, pound his stupid, ugly face in.

But he wouldn't, because he was afraid.

Finally, Russell crawled to the edge of the gutter, hoping desperately that the ring was still there, hadn't fallen into some unreachable place.

He couldn't spot it at first, and began to fear it had just mysteriously disappeared. But at last he noticed a bit of green sticking out of a small puddle. It was the upper edge of the monster-carved stone.

He picked up the ring, dried it on his shirt, then put it in his pocket.

He began to sob.

When the pain had diminished, he picked himself up and pedaled home to get ready for school all over again.

Russell's mother fussed over him as if his wounds had been made by bullets instead of fists.

"Why does this boy beat up on you, anyway, Russell?" she asked as she was driving him to school.

Russell shrugged. "He hates me."

"Why does he hate you?"

"He hates everyone, I guess."

"That's too bad. Why don't you try to make friends with him?"

Russell looked at his mother in astonishment. She had to be kidding. "Make friends with Eddie? He'd kill me, Ma."

"I don't think so, Russell. The next time he wants

to fight, just stick out your hand and say, 'Let's be friends.' You might be surprised at what happens."

"Yeah. Big surprise. He turns me into applesauce."

But Russell thought about his mother's words throughout the morning. One thing was certain: It would take as much guts to shake hands with Eddie as it would to punch him. Russell didn't think he could do it.

Anyway, he wasn't at all sure he *wanted* to make friends with someone who had just about killed him a few hours ago.

Russell's anger simmered within him through the day. And it was a long day. The hours seemed to drag. All he could think of was the party, and using the ring once more.

At last it was time to put on the costumes. Miss Snergal sent those kids who had a lot of changing to do out of the room.

Jack and Jimmy went with Russell to the big bathroom down the hall. (Jimmy had decided against being a pimple. He was dressing up like broccoli, instead. He said it was the most frightening thing he could think of.)

While Jack and Jimmy were putting on their costumes, Russell went into one of the toilet stalls. He slipped out of his school clothes, then donned the ragged shirt and trousers he had brought. Next he put on a pair of dirty, worn-down work boots that used to belong to his cousin Sidney. When everything was in place, he took out the ring and slipped it onto his finger.

He stared at it for a moment, wondering who had made it. The monster on top seemed to be looking back at him.

Suddenly Russell was more eager than ever to be a monster himself. His thoughts went back to that morning. Immediately his anger at Eddie welled up again. With it came an aching urge for revenge.

He made his decision.

Taking firm hold of the ring, Russell chanted the verse from the instruction sheet.

As he did, he turned the ring.

Twice.

✛

SIX

Double Whammy

Russell felt as if he had been kicked by a mule then dropped into a vat of ice water. Everything that had happened before was happening again, but twice as fast. He grew hot and cold by turns. There was a terrible itching under his skin, almost as if something were crawling around just beneath the surface. He could feel horns and hair bursting through.

Though he was vibrating with energy, he forced himself to wait. He couldn't leave the stall before the change was done. It wouldn't do to have Jack and Jimmy see his horns growing right before their eyes!

"Hey, Russell!" yelled Jack. "Hurry up! We're ready to go!"

"I'm coming," he growled. "Hold your horses."

He touched his horns. They had stopped growing. He looked at his hands. They were covered with thick black fur. Suddenly his fingernails began to morph into sharp claws. He watched them curl down from the fingertips, fierce and shiny.

He waited another moment, to see if there were any more changes, then stepped out of the stall.

"Holy Moses!" cried Jack. "That's incredible, Russell!"

"Where did you get it?" yelled Jimmy.

Russell was delighted to hear the jealousy in their voices. His "costume" was the kind of thing every kid dreamed of.

He shrugged. "I made it—from stuff we had around the house."

He sounded like a gorilla with a sore throat.

Jack and Jimmy gaped. "How did you do that voice?" Jack cried.

Russell smiled. "It's a secret."

He stepped to the mirror to examine himself and almost screamed.

He was ten times as ghastly now as he had been after the first change. His horns were longer and a brilliant fire-red. Hair sprang out all around his head, almost like a lion's mane. His nose was flat and shiny. And large fangs gleamed in his mouth—sharp things, deadly looking, made for ripping and tearing.

He remembered the lines on the instruction sheet:

Twist it once, you're horned and haired;
Twist it twice and fangs are bared.

But it was his eyes that really did the trick. They seemed to be twice their normal size and set more deeply into his head. Dark, evil-looking rings surrounded them, and thick, bloodshot lines ran in from the corners. Most incredible of all, the irises had turned red!

"Come on, Russell!" urged Jack. "I can't wait for Miss Snergal to see this!"

He threw his arm around Russell's shoulder. Jimmy did the same thing. This monster was theirs.

Russell was delighted. But as they were walking toward their classroom, something happened that should have made him worry. Without warning, without knowing why, he lifted his head and let out a long, mournful howl that echoed down the corridor.

Doors flew open and heads popped out as teachers looked for the source of the sound. Their faces were priceless. Jack almost fell over laughing, and Jimmy had to hold on to Russell's arm to support himself.

Outside their own room, they paused to prepare a grand entry. Jack swung the door open. Jimmy stepped in and bowed. "Ladies and gentlemen!" he cried. "Allow me to present to you the *real* Beast of Boardman Road!"

Russell was supposed to step into the room and stand there so everyone could ooh and ah over his fantastic costume. At least, that was the plan. Instead, without even intending to, he leaped through the door, growling ferociously. A second leap and he was crouching atop Missy Freebaker's desk, snarling fiercely. He turned warily about, baring his fangs, ready to attack the first thing that moved.

His effect on the class was electric. The girls

screamed, half of them because they loved screaming, the other half because they were genuinely frightened.

The boys squeaked.

Missy bolted from her desk and ran to Miss Snergal.

The teacher clapped her hands and suddenly the spell of terror was broken. "All right," she said. "That's enough. Settle down, everyone. Russell, that is certainly the most magnificent costume I have ever seen. But it does not justify this outrageous behavior. Get to your seat. *Now!*"

Russell shook his head. He looked around and saw the horrified faces of his classmates.

"Sorry, Miss Snergal. I got carried away."

She jumped at the sound of his voice.

"I should say so," she said, looking at him curiously.

Suddenly the class came to life. Before Russell could get down from the desk, they surged forward to examine him.

"Take off the mask, Russ!" said Georgie Smud. "I want to see how it fastens on."

"How'd you do the ears?" cried someone else.

"Where did you get those teeth?"

"Tell me how you put on the fur!"

"Now, class," said Miss Snergal, "perhaps Russell has some professional secrets that he would rather not divulge." She gave Russell a wink.

He smiled back, showing her a mouthful of fangs.

She looked startled, but went on addressing the

class. "Clear your desks, everyone. As soon as the parade's over, we'll have our party."

A cheer went up. Before long they were heading outside for the schoolwide costume parade. The kids not in costume were to sit on the curb of the traffic circle in front of the school while the rest of the kids—namely, all of the first and second graders, most of the thirds, about half of the fourths, and a handful of the fifths—went on parade to display their costumes.

Russell, Jack, and Jimmy took their places near the end of the line.

The parents cheered and clapped at Russell's "costume." But when Mr. Rafschnitz approached to award him first prize, the hair on the back of his neck stood up and his lip began to curl. A snarl was welling up in his throat and there was nothing he could do to stop it. Stretching out his claws, he began to snap at Mr. Rafschnitz.

The principal looked horrified—and it was not an act.

It was Jack who saved the day. Thinking that Russell was playing, he decided to get in on the fun. "Down, boy!" he shouted. "Down! Supper is waiting in the dungeon. Down. Down, beast!"

Russell gave Mr. Rafschnitz a snarl for good measure, accepted the blue ribbon, then let Jack lead him away.

"I've got to hand it to you, Russell," said Jack, once they were back inside. "You've got more guts than I have. No one else would have dared to growl at The Beast like that, not even Eddie."

They followed the class back to their room. When Russell bounded through the door, Mrs. Elmore, the room mother, took one look at him and almost dropped the tray of cookies she was carrying.

The party started. The kids swarmed to the goodies like starving hamsters let loose in a vegetable bin. But Russell wasn't interested. He did try a candy pumpkin, but it stuck in his fangs, and after that he just sat there growling and snorting.

It was the games that really started the trouble. The first hint of disaster came when they played Bite the Apple. Mrs. Elmore had threaded apples on strings and hung them from the ceiling. The kids were supposed to stand face-to-face and try to catch the apples with their teeth.

Russell was teamed with Frieda Mollis. When the apple slipped away from him, he got angry and started snapping at it. Then he started snapping at Frieda. She screamed. Miss Snergal ran over, crying, "Really, Russell, you must control yourself!"

"Sorry," he growled.

But he wasn't. He had enjoyed it. He wanted to growl and snap some more.

He wanted to run around and howl.

He wanted to scare the living daylights out of people!

And he got his chance. The next game was called Ugly Face. The class split into two lines facing each other. Then everyone had to make the ugliest face they could. Whoever laughed was out.

Russell thought this was a good idea. When the game started, he looked at Georgie Smud and curled his lips. Georgie didn't laugh. In fact, she looked scared. That was fine with Russell. He curled his lips even more and snarled. Georgie yelled. Russell began to jump up and down. He ran along the line, snarling and growling, trying to scare the entire other team at once.

"Russell!"

Miss Snergal again.

He held in his growl and bowed his head.

"Sorry."

"Just watch it." She turned to face the rest of the class. "I think it's time for the story."

Everyone cheered. Halloween was the best day of the year for stories, and Miss Snergal had already explained her plans to them.

First she drew the blinds and turned off the lights. Then she lit the jack-o'-lantern. Wrapping a cape around her shoulders, she hobbled to a corner and sat down. She crooked a finger and said in a creaky voice, "Come, children. Come to the Halloween corner to hear a tale of terror."

She was a good actress, and the combination of the dark, her voice, and the day made it easy to pretend that she really was a wicked witch.

"Once upon a time, there was a witch who lived in a cottage in the forest. Late at night, when the moon was high and shining on her hut, she would dance around her crackling fire and stir her bubbling cauldron."

Russell, who was sitting on a desk toward the back of the group, felt a howl begin to bubble inside him.

"One day a handsome prince came riding up to the cottage. He was dressed all in white and carried a sword at his side."

Russell's lip began to curl as he took an instant dislike to the handsome prince.

When the witch gave the prince a magic sword in place of his regular one and sent him on a quest for a monster, Russell began to squirm.

When Miss Snergal reached the part where the moon was full and the prince was riding into a great forest to find the monster and kill it, Russell felt as if he were going to jump out of his skin.

But it wasn't until the prince raised his sword to run the monster through that Russell finally broke. The howls and snarls that had been building up inside of him would wait no longer. Tipping back his head, he poured out a long, mournful wail.

Kill the monster, indeed!

✤

SEVEN

Russell Goes Berserk

Russell bounded off the desk. His heart was pounding, and the beast in his blood was going wild. Some of the kids screamed. Others began to edge away from him.

"Russell!" cried Miss Snergal. "Stop that this instant!" She stood up and flung off her cape. The story-telling witch was gone, replaced by an angry teacher.

Russell snarled at her.

Somewhere inside him, a tiny voice was crying, *This is crazy. Crazy! Stop it. Stop it NOW!*

But the monster part of him wouldn't listen.

His snarl deepened to a growl as he realized the one thing he really wanted to do:

Get Eddie!

With a roar, Russell charged out the door and across the hall to Mrs. Brown's room. Her door was closed, but monsters didn't bother to knock. He flung it open and burst through.

His entrance earned a squeal of terror from the kids.

Russell raised his arms and snarled.

All the kids—Eddie included—ran to the corner farthest from the door.

Mrs. Brown, who had been teaching for forty years, was not so easily intimidated. "Young man, you leave this room this instant!" she ordered.

Russell jumped onto a desk and howled.

"You heard me!" cried Mrs. Brown. "Get off that desk and out of my room!"

When Russell didn't move, she grabbed her broom and whacked him.

He yelped with rage and jumped down. But instead of fleeing the room, he headed for the corner where the children had huddled.

At that same instant, Miss Snergal staggered through the door.

"Russell!" she cried. "Stop!"

He glanced over his shoulder, hesitating for just a second. But it was too late. His prey was in striking range. He couldn't stop now. Raising his claws, he headed for Eddie.

"Oh no you don't!" yelled Mrs. Brown.

Then she hit him on the head with her broom.

Russell spun about in a blind fury.

Mrs. Brown whacked him again.

Half the children were laughing; the other half were crying.

Russell was roaring with outrage.

"Get out of here, whoever you are," snapped Mrs. Brown. "And don't come back!"

The Russell-monster hesitated, torn between getting at his enemy and getting away from the ferocious teacher.

He turned toward Eddie and snarled again.

Mrs. Brown swatted him across the backside.

That was enough, even for a monster. Russell started for the door. Mrs. Brown charged after him. "Out of my room, you ruffian!" she cried. "And stay out!"

Russell vaulted a desk, then shot past Miss Snergal, who looked as if she were about to faint. Entering the hall, he ran smack-dab into a class heading for its homeroom. He dashed into the middle of the group, growling and snarling.

The kids screamed and scattered.

He sped past them, raced down the hall, rounded the corner—and ran straight into another class!

He turned and headed back the way he had come.

From behind he heard someone cry, "Let's get him!"

He plunged back into the first class, which had just started to regroup. They slowed him down enough for the second class to catch up. Shrieking and giggling, kids began to pull at his fur, trying to remove the "costume."

Russell's monster side went wild. A huge, nearly unbelievable roar broke from his lungs.

The children shrank back, and he escaped. But almost instantly, both classes were after him again.

The wild rumpus attracted the children still in their rooms. Doors flew open. Heedless of their teachers' cries, kids poured into the hall to join the merry chase.

Merry for everyone but Russell. Yelping in fright, he was skidding around corners and down halls as fast as his powerful legs would carry him. But the floors were freshly waxed, and he slipped and slid and couldn't get a lead on his pursuers.

He dodged into the cafeteria.

The mob followed.

Russell took to the tabletops. Several great leaps carried him from one side of the lunchroom to the other. The pursuing mass of kids had to split and flow along the narrow spaces between the tables, which gained Russell time.

Just ahead of him was another door. A little way past that was a door to the outside, and freedom.

But standing in the first doorway, blocking Russell's path, was the original Beast of Boardman Road: Mr. Henry Rafschnitz himself!

For a moment Russell panicked. Then his monster side took over. Standing on the edge of a table, he gave a deep-throated roar, flexed his legs, and leaped straight at the principal.

Mr. Rafschnitz held his ground for an instant. Then, as he saw that the monster really intended to land on him, he dropped to the floor.

Russell shot over him and into the hall. He hurtled forward, flung open the big glass doors, and burst through to the golden afternoon.

Miss Snergal, who had somehow made it to the head of the chase, came running after him. Mr.

Rafschnitz grabbed the doors and locked the rest of the howling mob in.

"Russell!" cried Miss Snergal. "Russell, come back! I want to talk to you!"

But the sunlight was bringing him to his senses and he was terrified. Sprinting across the playground, he headed into the little wood that separated the school from the housing tract behind it. Scrambling up an old oak, he hid behind the scarlet leaves, where he leaned against the trunk, gasping for breath.

What had he just done?

He had to turn back to himself, and fast.

He looked down at the ring.

It was glowing!

Grabbing it with the claws of his left hand, he tried to twist it.

To his horror, it wouldn't budge.

Cold fear gripped his heart as he tried again. But his monster paws were larger than his hands had been, and the ring, which had moved so easily on his human finger, was too tight!

He tried again, straining mightily.

The ring seemed to clutch at his flesh. Fortunately, the increase in size that had made the ring so tight had also given him new strength. Locking his claws against the stone, he wrenched at it with all his might—then howled in pain as the ring finally moved on his finger.

Muttering the chant, he gave it two full turns.

Seconds later the beast was gone.

In its place sat Russell.

Quiet Russell, who had frightened four classes, snarled at two teachers, and terrified one principal.

Timid Russell, who had started the first riot in the history of Boardman Road Elementary School.

Quiet, timid Russell, who was in more trouble than he had ever dreamed of in his entire life.

✜

EIGHT

The Beast Within

School was over, and the buses had all left. Russell was still hiding in the tree. Just as he was wondering if he should climb down—and what he could possibly do next if he did—he heard the dreaded sound: "Russseelllll! Russsseeellllll Crannaker!"

They had called his mother.

Russell sighed. Now things might get *really* scary.

He considered his choices.

One: He could tell the truth.

Two: He could run away from home and become a tramp.

Three: He could get sick and throw up all over.

None of them seemed like a good idea.

Well, sooner or later he had to climb out of the tree, walk back to the school, and face his mother (not to mention Miss Snergal and Beast Rafschnitz).

It might as well be now.

Moving slowly, he returned to the ground.

Emerging from the woods, he spotted his mother standing at the edge of the playground. Her perpetually worried look was accentuated by her current upset over whatever the school had already told her.

She caught sight of him, waved, and hurried forward. "Russell, are you all right? Miss Snergal called and told me some terrible story about you going crazy and causing a riot. The woman must be losing her mind. 'My Russell?' I said. 'My boy, cause a riot?' I know you could never have done all the things she said."

Russell felt his fear begin to shift into quiet anger. Why *couldn't* he have done those things? He was no baby. He was just as capable of misbehaving as any other kid in the school.

But he didn't say anything.

"It was that terrible Eddie, wasn't it?" continued Mrs. Crannaker. "I'm going to speak to Mr. Rafschnitz about him first thing Monday morning. It's not right to have him after you like that. You're a delicate child. It makes you nervous." She paused for breath, then said, "Well, come with me. Mother will get everything fixed up."

Russell maintained a stony silence. But he could feel an uncomfortable urge to lash out at his mother building inside him. His resentment at being babied was growing stronger with every word she uttered.

The school was empty. They stopped in the boys' room to pick up his clothing, and then in his classroom so they could collect his books. A pile of candy and a cupcake had been neatly arranged on his desk, an unspoken message of forgiveness from Miss Snergal.

His mother shivered at the sight. "Throw that garbage away," she commanded. "Thank goodness you didn't eat it!"

Russell hesitated, then gathered the goodies and carried them to the trash can.

The ride home was ghastly. Russell was on the verge of telling his mother exactly how he felt. But somehow he couldn't get started. It was as if all his feelings, and the words for those feelings, were in a bottle with a little cork at the top. But the cork wouldn't come loose.

He hunched into himself and stared out the window. Inside he felt stronger and braver and more ready to tell people what he thought than he ever had before.

He just didn't feel brave enough to try it on his mother.

It wasn't until later that night that he realized how weird the situation was: He had been dreading getting in trouble—and now he was annoyed because his mother was refusing to believe he had done anything wrong!

The next morning Russell scrambled out of bed with unusual energy. It was Halloween, and he was impatient for the night, though the day had hardly begun.

He sailed down the stairs and into the kitchen. Breakfast was ready. He took his place at the table.

"I want to talk to you, Russell."

He froze, a spoonful of oatmeal halfway to his mouth.

His mother was looking at him intently.

"About yesterday."

He put down the spoon.

"I talked to Jack's mother this morning. She said Jack told her you really did act like a maniac in school yesterday. Why did he say that, Russell?"

Russell sighed. No sense in hiding it now. "Because it's true."

His mother looked astonished, and hurt. "It can't be! I know you better than that. You could never misbehave so badly."

Russell felt his anger of the day before return. What did she think he was, a plastic angel? He thrust out his chin, about to tell his mother everything. Then he looked at her, and saw how her eyes were pleading with him to say he hadn't done it.

More to the point, they were telling him she wouldn't believe him even if he had.

He sighed. "You're right, Mom. It isn't true. I don't know why Jack said that. I think he's mad at me. All the kids are out to get me. They all hate me."

He was so convincing that he almost began to feel sorry for himself.

"There, there, Russell," said Mrs. Crannaker.

Russell didn't know whether it was funny or sad that it was easier for his mother to believe that the whole class was picking on him than it was for her to believe he had misbehaved.

She put her arm around his shoulder and patted him. "I'll talk to Miss Snergal first thing Monday. Don't worry. Mother will make it better."

He pushed away from her smothering embrace. "I don't want you to make it better!" he cried. "Why won't you ever let me make something better myself?"

It was hard to tell which of them was more shocked. His mother looked at him with hurt eyes. Her lip began to tremble. Russell pushed away from the table and ran from the house.

He plopped down in a little park about two blocks from home. Sitting beneath a large oak tree, he clenched his fists and began to pound the piles of dead leaves that surrounded him.

He picked up an acorn and threw it.

Why did his mother treat him like such a baby?

He threw another acorn.

How could he grow up if he never got the chance?

He threw a third acorn.

"Ouch!"

Russell looked up.

Not ten feet away, standing astride his bicycle, was Eddie. He had a strange look on his face—a combination of anger, amusement, and (could it be?) fear. He paused, then hopped off his bike and sauntered over to where Russell sat.

"That was some outfit you had on in school yesterday, Crannaker. Made you feel pretty brave, didn't it?"

"Oh, go play in the road, toad," said Russell.

Eddie's face tightened, and Russell saw him begin to ball his hands into fists. "What did you say, Crannaker?"

"You heard me, peabrain. Go lick your finger and stick it in a socket."

Russell nearly laughed out loud at the look on Eddie's face. It occurred to him that he was doing something very dangerous. It also occurred to him that he didn't care.

Eddie stepped closer.

Russell stood up. For the first time he could remember, he made a fist with the intention of using it on someone. He had a feeling he was going to get pounded again. But this time he was going to pound back.

Suddenly he wasn't sure he wanted to. Fighting was stupid.

He tightened his fists, anyway, and brought them up against his sides. He could feel a snarl creeping up his throat. This was exciting! Suddenly he wanted to howl, had an urge to leap on Eddie with claws and fangs going all at once.

That scared him.

He looked at his hands, half expecting them to be sprouting fur.

He took a deep breath, lowered his fists, and said, "Look, Eddie, I don't want to fight..."

"Of course you don't," sneered Eddie. "You're a chicken! *Bawk ba bawk ba bawk.*"

He pushed Russell's shoulder.

It wasn't a hard push. But it made something inside Russell snap.

"You idiot!" he roared.

Then he jumped.

Eddie's eyes went wide. He cried out in fear.

Russell had become a whirlwind of thrashing arms and flailing legs. Eddie toppled beneath his onslaught. Holding his enemy down, Russell opened his mouth to take a bite out of Eddie's shoulder.

That's when the warning bell went off in his head.

"What am I doing?" he cried in horror.

Terrified now, not of Eddie but of himself, he leaped to his feet and raced off. He ran for blocks, afraid that if he stopped, something awful would happen.

At last his body forced him to halt. Panting, gasping, he leaned against a building and let the question rage through his brain: *What was this ring doing to him?*

He could think of only one place to go for an answer.

Mr. Elives' magic shop.

Three hours later, baffled and exhausted, Russell had to admit that there was one problem with this idea: He couldn't find the darn place!

After the first hour of searching, he had returned to the alley where he had played at being Frankenstein's monster the afternoon he had first found the shop. From there he tried to retrace his flight from Eddie. But somehow he kept getting turned around.

He had just ended up back at the alley for the fourth time, and was trying to decide whether to be frightened or angry, when a small voice said, "Hey, kid!"

Russell looked around.

"Down here!" said the voice. "On the trash can."

He looked down.

Standing on the lid of a battered metal garbage can were two rats. One of them reared up on its hind legs and said, "Are you Russell Crannaker?"

Russell stared at the creature in astonishment.

"What's the matter?" asked the rat. "Cat got your tongue?" It slapped its sides in amusement. "Oh, that's a good one. 'Cat got your tongue?' I kill me."

"For heaven's sake, Jerome," said the other rat—a female, judging by her voice. "Don't you think that joke is getting a little worn-out?"

"Aw, come on, Roxanne," said the first rat sullenly. "I was just having a little fun."

She glared at him.

Jerome sighed. Turning back to Russell, he said, "Okay, kid, just answer the question. Is your name Russell Crannaker, or not?"

"What if it is?" said Russell warily.

Now the female rat stood up. "If it is, then we have a message for you."

✜

NINE

The Third Twist
of the Ring

Russell stared at the rats. He was tempted to twist the ring; only, turning into a monster to deal with a pair of talking rats seemed like overkill.

"What's the message?" he asked, his voice almost as squeaky as that of the rats.

It was the second rat, the female, who answered. "Mr. Elives said to stop bothering him."

"I'm not bothering him," said Russell in astonishment. "I can't even find him!"

"You think he doesn't know you're looking?" asked the first rat. "It really bugs him when people do that. And trust me, kid, Elives is not a guy you want to bug if you don't have to."

"But I need to talk to him! I have to ask him about this ring."

"Did you read the directions carefully?" asked Roxanne.

"Yes."

"Then you don't need to ask him anything," said Jerome. "As long as you pay close attention to them—"

"He asked us to remind you of that," interrupted Roxanne.

Jerome scowled at her. "As long as you pay close attention to the directions, you've got everything you need to know. If Elives wants to tell you something else, he'll get word to you one way or another."

The rats started down the side of the garbage can.

"Wait!" said Russell. "How come you can talk?"

"It's a long story," said Roxanne, once she had reached the ground. "And we have work to do. The old man keeps us pretty busy—especially at this time of the year."

She turned and scampered after Jerome.

"Wait!" cried Russell again. But it was too late. He watched helplessly as the rats disappeared through a crack in the alley wall.

Two hours later, Russell sat in his room, staring at the ring.

It scared him. Oh, he loved it—loved the monstrous carving, and the magic that it contained. But he was frightened by what was happening to him. Not to mention the fact that he was now having conversations with rats.

He looked at the ring again. So far it had gotten him into more trouble than he was willing to think about.

The thing was, it had also been a lot of fun.

Should he use it tonight, or not?

Common sense was saying no.

But another side of him, a wilder side, was saying, "It's *Halloween*! What better time to be a monster?"

He *had* been looking forward to this night all week.

He glanced at the instruction sheet lying on his desk.

Twist it once, you're horned and haired;
Twist it twice and fangs are bared;
Twist it thrice? No one has dared!

He *had* felt very daring lately.

He smiled. One good thing—he didn't have to make up his mind right away. With the ring he could put on his "costume" anytime he wanted to.

He put the directions in an envelope. Going to his dresser, he opened the center drawer. Lifting out a stack of underwear—each pair carefully labeled by his mother for the day of the week that he was to wear it—he put the envelope in the bottom of the drawer for safekeeping. He replaced the underwear, then went downstairs.

His mother was in the den, reading a cookbook.

"I'm going to the bonfire now," he said.

"All right, Russell. Have a good time."

He stared at her in surprise. Her expression was blank, emotionless. He wasn't sure if she was still hurt over what had happened this morning, or if this was a new way of punishing him for that outburst.

He sighed, feeling the delight of the moment drain away.

Quietly, he left the house.

Every year the town council held a bonfire at the high school to keep the kids out of mischief on Halloween. They organized games, served cider and doughnuts, and gave prizes for the best costumes. It was a good time and Russell always looked forward to it.

This year Kennituck Falls had a perfect night for the celebration. A wild October wind was blowing through the trees, chasing dead leaves around their trunks. The sky was clear, sprinkled with stars. You could almost smell the magic in the air.

Russell nabbed a cup of cider, crammed half a doughnut into his mouth, and wandered through the happy crowd to see how the bobbing for apples was going. Suddenly he spotted Eddie out of the corner of his eye. His enemy was in the grip of a large, mean-looking teenager. From the frightened expression that twisted Eddie's face, Russell could tell that he was feeling the same kind of fear that he, Russell, had so often felt when trapped in Eddie's grasp.

Watching as the older boy steered Eddie through the crowd, Russell decided to follow. He trailed the two boys around the corner of the school, pressing himself to the building so that he wouldn't be seen. Once they were away from the bonfire, the darkness grew more intense.

Two other teenagers stepped from the shadows. "You got him!" cried one, happily.

The others shushed him.

Russell edged closer to the four figures, listening intently.

"Aw, come on, you guys," whined Eddie. "I didn't do anything that bad."

Russell recognized the nervous edge in Eddie's voice; he had heard it often enough in his own.

"Of course you didn't," sneered one of the boys. "We just want to teach you a lesson now, before you do anything worse."

Another reached into Eddie's shirt pocket. "Here's his soap. He was gonna soap more windows."

"Maybe we should soap *him*," said the third boy. "How about that, punk? Wanna take a bath in the river?"

"Yeah. And then you can play Find Your Clothes," said the first with a laugh.

Russell began to get edgy. He rubbed his thumb against the ring.

Eddie made a break for it. The biggest of the boys grabbed him.

"Help!" cried Eddie.

"Shut up, punk!" snapped the boy. He slapped Eddie sharply.

That did it. Russell, infuriated by seeing even his enemy get bullied, began to twist the ring, repeating the chant as he did. Once, twice—and then, in the heat of his anger, a third time.

A small explosion rocked his head. He knew at

once, with a deep conviction, that this change was going to be very different from the ones that had come before it.

The boys were dragging Eddie off. Russell started to follow, then staggered and fell back into the shadow of a doorway. The change was coming too fast, too strong. He couldn't move.

All the familiar things were happening: the horns, the fangs, the hair on hands and feet. But something else—something strange and new—was happening, too. He felt as if someone had reached inside of him, grabbed his toes, and was trying to turn him inside out.

He was hot and cold by alternate flashes.

A foul odor was emanating from his skin.

Suddenly he was scared, scared to the bottom of his soul.

"No one has dared!" the instructions had said.

Had he gone too far?

He became aware of a stabbing pain in his back. It increased in intensity until he fell to the ground, writhing in agony. A sudden rush of even more intense pain, sharp and flamelike . . . a tearing sound . . . a feeling that he was being ripped apart . . . and then the impossible happened.

Up from his shoulders sprang two huge, batlike wings.

But there was no time to think about that miracle. The heat from his body had become unbearable. Lifting himself to his hands and knees, Russell saw the hair on the backs of his hands begin to smoke.

The heat grew more intense. He realized with sudden horror that his clothes were smoking, too. Desperate, he tore at them. Too late. They had reached the flash point.

In one horrible moment, Russell Crannaker was wrapped in flames from head to toe.

✣

TEN

Russell to the Rescue

Russell cried out in terror and flung himself to the ground, ready to roll in an attempt to extinguish the flames. But as quickly as they had begun, they died away.

He lay there for a moment, too stunned to think. Then a stray beam of moonlight struck his hand, and he gasped at what he saw, the strange change in his skin.

Yet the moonlight itself seemed to calm him, offer him new strength.

He pushed himself to his knees, then slowly rose to his feet, stretching his arms to the beckoning silver circle above him. And if he had been a monster before, Russell Crannaker was a king among monsters now. His entire body was covered with overlapping red scales that gleamed like burnished metal. His wings stretched tall behind him, their peaks and points looming against the night. And in his eyes there burned a fire that could freeze a man with fear.

He beat his fists against his chest, then extended his wings, flapped them twice, and floated into the air.

Even though it was his own strength that lifted him, Russell felt an instant of panic. It was as if he had been plucked from the earth, was being carried away by some giant winged beast.

Except the beast was him.

The panic gave way to a surge of delight.

Working the wings with his powerful shoulder muscles, he rose into the night, into the deep black heavens. The ground shrank away as he drew level with the treetops. He continued to rise, on and up, toward the mysterious moon.

I wonder how high I can go? he thought—then decided to find out. But when he had soared to about three hundred feet, he looked down and suddenly felt as if he had just taken a dive on the biggest roller coaster in the world. His stomach began begging for mercy.

He dropped back to about a hundred feet, then began to glide lazily over the town.

He found it deeply satisfying to be flying through the night under his own power. The silence—no sound save the wind on his wings—made it seem as if he had entered another world, separate from the one that drifted below him, so very far away.

Passing over the high school, Russell was attracted by the bonfire. Three or four hundred costumed children, looking like beetles, milled about, happily guzzling cider and gobbling doughnuts.

With a roar, Russell swooped down toward them. He was rewarded with a flurry of exclamations, pointing, and screaming.

Just as quickly, he soared away again, over the top of the school, leaving them wondering but happy. Most of them would remember this Halloween as the best of their lives.

A few blocks past the school, Russell suddenly spotted four figures—three large ones and a smaller one—struggling wildly.

Eddie and his teenage attackers!

Russell had forgotten them in the heat of his transformation. But it was clear that Eddie was in big trouble. And despite all the bullying Eddie had done to him in the past, three against one stuck in Russell's throat.

Without giving him time to think, his monster side snapped into action.

First came an earsplitting roar. Thundering through the night, it spun the teenagers around.

Their eyes bulged with horror, as if they were seeing the end of the world. Actually, as far as they were concerned, they were. For as Russell flew toward them, he looked like nothing so much as death on wings, descending now to claim them.

"*Move!*" screamed one.

Dropping Eddie, they raced for safety.

That should have been enough; Eddie was out of danger. But Russell's hunting spirit was roused. He shot after the older boys like an arrow from a bow. Working his huge, batlike wings, he sped along a mere five feet above the pavement. His blood pounded through his veins, afire with the joy of the chase.

An instant later, he closed on the boy in the rear.

"Gotcha!" snarled Russell as he caught the teenager under the arms with his claws.

Changing direction, he headed straight up.

"Helllllp!" screamed his captive. "Let me down! Let me down!"

He squirmed and began to kick wildly.

"Careful," growled Russell, "or I might drop you."

Then he chuckled.

The frightened teenager looked down.

They were at least a hundred feet above the street.

He stopped kicking.

Russell, thrilled with the strength in his usually puny arms, continued to rise. Soon they were higher than the tallest building in the town. The land had become like a map beneath them: the houses, small boxes; the streets, little lines. The moon sparkled on the river at the west edge of town.

Russell swooped toward the black and silver water. "How would you like a bath?" he asked, remembering how the boys had threatened Eddie.

The memory triggered another idea. As long as he was at it, maybe he ought to give *Eddie* a good scare. Not hurt him, as these jokers had intended. Just... educate him a little.

Suddenly he lost interest in the rowdy dangling from his talons.

"Remember this the next time you decide to pick on someone," Russell growled. Swooping even lower, he dropped the boy in the mud at the river's edge. The teenager made a satisfying *sploosh* as he landed.

Russell rose again, banked in a sharp curve, and zoomed back toward where he had left Eddie.

He wasn't there. It took Russell a few minutes, but searching was easier when you could fly. He soon located his old nemesis cowering in the back entrance of the high school, a glazed expression on his face.

Russell landed about fifteen feet in front of him. "There you are!" he said, in booming tones. "I've been looking for you!"

Eddie jumped up, pressing himself against the locked door. "Get away from me! Get away, you monster!"

"Be quiet," snarled Russell.

"Right," said Eddie. "Anything you say." He was so tight against the door he looked as if he were trying to squeeze through the keyhole.

"Now listen," said Russell. "You've been picking on a friend of mine, and I want it to stop."

Eddie looked blank. "Who?" he asked at last.

"Russell Crannaker. I want you to leave him alone."

The look on Eddie's face changed to pure astonishment.

Russell bared his fangs, hissing as he did.

"Right," said Eddie quickly. "I leave him alone, and you leave me alone. Right?"

"You've got it," said Russell. "But don't forget, or..." He paused, looking for a stern enough threat, but finally ended with, "...or you'll be very, *very* sorry."

It seemed to do the trick. "I won't," whimpered Eddie. "I *promise!*"

Roaring with laughter, Russell flapped his wings and soared back into the night sky. He flew until he was out of Eddie's sight, then settled beside a tree in Stearns Park. He was still chuckling. Frightening Eddie like that was the most satisfying thing he had ever done. Now to change back—and test Eddie's resolution to leave him alone.

He grasped the ring. As before, it was hard to turn. But his claws were strong. He twisted it on his finger, said the familiar words, and waited.

Nothing happened.

✦

ELEVEN

Partners

Russell couldn't believe it.

He must have done something wrong.

He tried again.

Nothing—absolutely nothing.

He tried again . . . and again . . . and again.

It was no use. The ring wasn't working!

Now what?

The directions. He had to get the directions!

Stretching his leathery wings, Russell soared into the air and headed for home.

To his relief, the backyard was empty. Folding his wings, he dropped straight down, then extended them just in time to break the fall. Gliding silently to his bedroom, he stuck his head through the window.

That was *all* he could stick through! No matter how he folded his wings behind him, they were too big to pass through the frame.

Now what?

Heart pounding with panic, he flew away from the house. His mind was working even faster than his wings. But he couldn't think of what to do—until he spotted Eddie staggering along the street below him.

Russell flew ahead. He landed on the roof of one of the buildings, then climbed down the wall to hide in the alley—the same alley, he suddenly realized, where he had played at being Frankenstein's monster, and where he had recently had a conversation with two rats.

He waited in the shadows at the mouth of the alley, then called Eddie's name as he walked past.

"What do you want now?" screamed Eddie. "I told you I'd leave Russell alone."

"I have to talk to you," said Russell, trying to keep his voice from booming too much. "Step in here."

Eddie hesitated.

Russell let a growl rumble in his throat, then said, "I can fly faster than you can even *think* of running. If I wanted to catch you, I could have done it anytime. I want to talk to you. Now get in here!"

Eddie stepped into the alley.

"Follow me," said Russell, then walked farther along the alley so that they would be out of sight of the street. When he felt they were in a safe spot, he turned and said, "I saved you from those teenagers, right?"

"Yes . . ."

"So you know I'm not going to hurt you, right?"

Eddie hesitated, then said, "I guess so."

"Okay, now I'm going to tell you something else. Remember how I said Russell Crannaker was a friend of mine?"

Eddie nodded.

"That wasn't the whole story." He paused, then said, "Eddie, I *am* Russell."

Eddie looked blank.

"This is me, Eddie. Russell. Russell Crannaker!"

Eddie stared at him incredulously. "What do you mean, you're Russell? That's impossible!"

"Do you remember yesterday in school?" asked Russell.

"You mean when Russell wore that crazy costume and...and..." A look of astonishment blossomed in Eddie's eyes. *"You mean that wasn't a costume?"*

Russell shook his monstrous head from side to side.

Eddie turned even paler. His eyes got wider. His lips worked, but the only sound that came out was "Buh...buh...buh..."

He looked like a goldfish.

Russell smiled. It was clear that Eddie had just decided he'd been taking his life in his hands every time he bothered poor, puny Russell Crannaker.

Finally, Eddie found his voice. "H-h-how come you let me get away with all that stuff?"

He squeaked. It was pathetic.

Inspiration struck. Shrugging his great wings, Russell said, "Punks like you don't bother me. I have more important things to worry about."

He was inwardly delighted. That offhand dismissal should finish convincing Eddie that Russell could have destroyed him at any time.

It ought to keep him safe for the rest of his life.

If he ever got to *be* Russell again!

He became aware that Eddie was talking. "...so thanks for saving me from those guys."

"It was nothing. I just didn't like their style." Trying to sound casual, he added, "But as long as you appreciated it, there *is* something you could do to help me in return."

"Sure," said Eddie quickly. "Anything."

"There's something I need in my room. It's not easy for me to get it until I change back. So I want you to get it for me."

"No problem," said Eddie. "Just tell me how to get in."

"I'll fly you there."

Eddie blanched.

"What's the matter?" asked Russell dryly. "You're not chicken, are you? *Bawk ba bawk ba bawk.*"

"No! It's just that...No, I'm not afraid. Let's go."

"Okay," said Russell.

He stepped forward. Eddie cowered back again.

"If I wanted to hurt you, I would have done it already," said Russell. "Now turn around."

Eddie did as he was told. Russell hooked his powerful hands under Eddie's arms, flapped his wings, and lifted into the air.

"Wow!" said Eddie. "This is great. How did you get like this, anyway?"

"None of your business!" snapped Russell.

"Sorry," said Eddie meekly.

When they reached the house, Russell coasted to the window and put Eddie on the sill.

"Now listen," he hissed. "In the middle drawer of that dresser there's a small white envelope. Get it for me."

The fierce insistence in his voice was all the motivation Eddie needed. He scrambled through the window, then scooted to the dresser and pulled open the drawer.

He turned back to the window, a puzzled expression on his face. "Why does your underwear say Tuesday on it?"

"Never mind that!" snapped Russell. "Just get the envelope. Fast!"

Socks and underwear flew in all directions as Eddie scrabbled through the drawer in search of the envelope.

"I don't see it," he whispered.

Russell snarled dangerously. "Keep looking!"

Eddie redoubled his efforts. As he did, they heard the sound of footsteps in the hall.

Eddie's head whipped around. "Someone's coming!"

"Keep looking!" ordered Russell again. "I have to have that envelope!"

Eddie was wild with fear, a far different fear than he had shown at the sight of Russell. "If I get caught here, I'll be arrested!"

"LOOK!" roared Russell.

Eddie scooped out the last contents of the drawer, then jumped up in triumph. "Got it!" he shouted, waving the envelope.

The doorknob rattled.

"Jump!" ordered Russell.

Eddie sprinted for the window and dove through headfirst.

✦

TWELVE

Return to the Magic Shop

For a sickening instant, Russell was not certain he could catch Eddie. But his powerful arms did the job almost instinctively. Snatching him up in midfall, Russell soared into the sky, Eddie dangling and gasping below him.

"Good grief!" panted Eddie.

"Good job," said Russell. "I'll remember it."

Mr. Crannaker stuck his head out the window, craning his neck as he scanned the ground to catch sight of whoever had just been in the room.

As Russell expected, it never occurred to his dad to look up.

When he had flown far enough from the house, he said to Eddie, "Where do you want me to drop you off?"

"Home will be fine," said Eddie weakly.

Russell felt a pang at the words, since he wanted nothing more than to go home himself.

"You'll have to tell me the way," he said, realizing that he had no idea where Eddie lived.

"It's the west side of town—across the river."

They flew over the sparkling silver water, so high above it they could scarcely hear the sound of the little falls by the old paper mill.

Following Eddie's directions, Russell landed in a vacant lot.

"My house is over that way," said Eddie. "I'll walk from here."

Russell had no idea which house it was, but he realized that all the houses here were small and shabby.

"Well, I guess this is it," said Eddie. "Thanks again for saving me from those guys."

"Not a problem," said Russell. "Thanks for getting that envelope for me."

He held out his scaly hand. Eddie passed him the envelope. Russell took it delicately between his claws. He tried to slip it into his pocket, then remembered that he didn't have one. He tucked it under his arm, instead, then held out his hand again.

Eddie looked at it for a moment, then put out his own hand to shake. "Well, see you in school," he said. He turned to go, then turned back and said, "Sorry about all that...well, you know. But we're square now, right?"

"We're square," said Russell.

Eddie nodded, and seemed to relax just a bit. Then he turned and walked away.

Russell watched him go, feeling confident that his troubles with Eddie were finally over.

On the other hand, Eddie was the least of his worries now.

He took to the sky again, looking for a place where he could think without interruption—without danger of being seen.

Finally he landed on the flat, empty roof of the high school, which was ringed by a low wall about eight inches high.

The bonfire had been extinguished. The crowd had vanished. The night was quiet, save for the sound of the rising wind. The silvery light shifted and changed as the moon went in and out of hiding among the clouds.

Russell stared at the envelope, almost afraid to open it. He was more and more troubled by the memory of one line in the instructions: "Twist it thrice? No one has dared!"

Had that been a challenge, as he had believed— or a warning?

His heart turned cold at the thought.

With trembling fingers, he extracted the crumpled paper. Unfolding it was not easy—claws were not made for this kind of work. But when he finally held it open, the moonlight, shining over his shoulder, struck another line that he had ignored, one vitally important instruction he hadn't even considered in his rush to save Eddie from the teenagers.

"Use with caution, *and never on the night of a full moon.*"

He looked over his shoulder.

Hanging in the sky above him was the silver circle

of the moon—fuller, it now seemed, than he had ever seen it before.

Never on the night of a full moon.

With a dead thump of certainty, he realized that he had made the ghastliest mistake of his life—three twists of a magic ring on the night of a great full moon.

He was ruined. There was no way out—no way to become plain old Russell Crannaker again.

Now that he thought about it, being plain old Russell Crannaker wasn't all that bad. He had a good home and loving parents. He had some friends. He did well in school. He had a teacher he enjoyed.

And it was gone, all gone, because he had been fool enough to use the ring—and use it to excess—on the night of a full moon.

Fool moon, they should call it.

"I'm the fool!" cried Russell, shaking his fists at the sky.

"Oh, I wouldn't go that far," replied a tiny but familiar voice.

He looked down.

The two rats he had met in the alley were standing on the edge of the low wall.

"How did you get here?" he cried.

"It wasn't easy," said Roxanne. "We've been chasing you all over town."

"Why?"

"Why?" asked Jerome in astonishment. "How about, you did something so stupid no one can believe it?"

"Oh, stop, Jerome," said Roxanne. "The boy doesn't need you to tell him how foolish he was. He's figured that much out on his own."

"Just trying to clarify the situation," muttered Jerome.

"If you want to clarify things, tell me how to turn back!" growled Russell.

"What do we look like?" asked Jerome. "Magicians?"

"Did you come here just to torment me?" asked Russell bitterly.

"To advise you," said Roxanne gently.

"What's your advice?" asked Russell, trying to keep his temper from erupting again.

"That you should get some help," said Jerome.

"That doesn't take a genius," said Russell. "But where am I going to get it?"

"Where did you get the ring?" countered Roxanne.

"At the magic shop. But I already tried to find it again, and you two told me to stop looking for it."

"That was before you got yourself into this mess," said Roxanne.

"Which really took some first-class boneheadery," added Jerome with a chuckle.

Roxanne poked him in the ribs. "Oh, be quiet, Jerome."

"Look, just tell me how to find the shop," pleaded Russell.

Roxanne shook her head. "Think, Russell. What can you do now that you couldn't do the last time you looked for the shop?"

Russell considered for a moment. Then the answer hit him. "I can fly!" he cried. "Maybe I can spot it from above!" He climbed onto the edge of the roof, then turned back to thank the rats.

They were nowhere in sight.

Shaking his head, Russell stretched his wings and leaped into the night air.

For the next hour, he flew back and forth above Kennituck Falls, searching desperately for any sign of the shop. Time and again he returned to the alley where he had played at being Frankenstein's monster. He would start above the place where Eddie had slipped on the garbage and try to retrace his route. The first five or six times he failed, lost the track. Then, just when his despair was deepest, he flew into a patch of fog.

When he came out the other side, he saw the street of little shops. And at the end of the street... There it was: the magic shop!

Russell landed in front of the shop, filled with a sense of relief.

He glanced stealthily up and down the street.

Deserted.

What time was it, anyway? His parents must be out of their minds with worry. But what could he do? Walk in and say, "Hi, Mom! Hi, Dad! It's me—Russell. What happened to my skin? Oh, I made a little mistake with this magic ring I've been messing around with, and I'm going to be a monster from now on. You don't mind, do you?"

He realized, for good and all, that if he could not

reverse this change, he would never see home and parents again. A sob forced its way through his monsterish throat, a sound it had never been formed to make.

He pounded on the door. A light went on in the back of the shop. Russell glanced around, afraid his racket would rouse someone else, too.

The empty street emboldened him.

"Let me in!" he shouted, pounding on the door with both fists now. "Let me in!"

"I'm coming," called a familiar voice, sounding deeply cranky. "I'm coming. Pipe down."

Russell peered through the window. The old man who had sold him the ring was shuffling toward the door, carrying an old-fashioned candleholder. He wore a ratty-looking bathrobe, covered with moons and stars, and tattered carpet slippers that kept sliding off his heels.

The door snapped open. "What are you trying to do, raise the dead? There's enough of them up and around already tonight!"

The old man paused as his eyes focused on Russell. Quickly he grabbed the monster's arm and pulled him into the shop.

Then he slammed the door behind him.

"So it's you," he said, with just a hint of smugness in his voice. "I've been expecting you."

"What?"

"Oh, come, come. You hardly struck me as being the careful type when I sold you that ring. Hardly the type to pay attention to . . . vital instructions?"

Russell, the beast of a thousand nightmares, looked at the floor in shame.

"Well," said Mr. Elives sharply, "what have you come for?"

Russell looked up in astonishment. "I want you to help me."

Mr. Elives flung up his hands in disgust. "I sold you the ring, didn't I? What more do you want?"

"I want to change back!"

"That's hardly my concern. I included very specific directions with that ring. I even sent a pair of messengers to remind you to read them carefully. The terms were very clear: Never use the ring on the night of a full moon. You can read, can't you?"

"Yes, of course, but—"

"But, but, but! Directions are directions. You follow them or you don't. What you choose to do with a thing once I sell it to you is none of my concern. If you can't be responsible for your actions, you can hardly expect *me* to take responsibility for them."

"But—"

"And furthermore, it is highly inconsiderate to come to my shop at this hour and rouse me out of a sound sleep. I work hard all day, and I don't need some fool who can't follow directions coming around in the middle of the night to disturb my rest."

Russell knew that if his monster self could cry, he would be crying by now. But he wouldn't be ashamed of it this time. He had been wrong, really wrong.

He said the only thing he could think of.

"I'm sorry."

"Well, in that case," said Mr. Elives, "sit down for a minute. We'll talk." He motioned to a chair. Russell cleared away a top hat and a string of silk scarves and sat down, his wings spread on either side of the chair.

"You cast a nice shadow," said Mr. Elives approvingly.

Russell looked around at the peaked and pointed shadow made by his wings. "I'd just as soon get rid of it," he said softly.

"I'm well aware of that. Now, tell me. How many times have you used the ring?"

"Three."

"One twist, then two, and finally three?"

Russell nodded.

The old man scratched his chin. "Most people are bright enough to stop at two."

Russell blushed, but it was hidden by his flame red cheeks.

"And on the night of a full moon." Mr. Elives shook his head and sighed. "Well," he said at last, "you'll have to stay in that shape for a while."

Russell looked up with sudden hope. "A while?"

Mr. Elives nodded. "With a ring like that, there's no way the counterspell can take effect on the night of a full moon. She has powers of her own, you know. But things may be different tomorrow. Time has a way of doing that."

"Of doing what?"

"Of changing things," said the old man. "Of course, not all change is for the better." He shrugged. "You'll just have to wait and see. Now, if you'd like to spend the rest of the night here, you can sleep in that chair."

"Thank you," said Russell. He hesitated, then said, "Do you have a phone I can use?"

The old man looked at him in astonishment. "What kind of a place do you think this is?" he demanded indignantly.

"But I need to call my parents. What am I going to tell them?"

"Tell them anything you want! I can't solve all your problems for you!" He paused, then added, "And don't come running back to me if there are any aftereffects, either."

Russell looked up, about to ask what he meant. But the man had turned and was heading toward the curtain that covered the door behind the counter.

Russell sighed and leaned back in the chair.

He would deal with all that when he came to it.

Right now he only wanted to sleep.

✦

THIRTEEN

Home Run

Russell woke with a start.

The cold gray light of morning was leaking through the window.

He looked down at his body. *His body!* He had it back. He was himself again!

He let out a whoop of joy.

"Be quiet!" yelled Mr. Elives from the back of the shop. "I'm trying to sleep!"

Russell held in his excitement. But it wasn't easy. He wanted to sing—shout—dance. He was Russell Crannaker, fifth-grade boy, and Russell-the-monster was gone, gone, gone.

Then he realized he had a new problem.

His clothes had been burned off during his transformation the night before.

He was stark naked!

Now what was he going to do?

He sat for a moment, pondering the question.

Finally, gathering his courage, he stepped behind the counter and went to the curtain.

He noticed the owl that sat on the cash register looking at him.

"Mind your own business," he whispered, feeling himself blush. Ignoring the bird, he pulled aside the curtain and said softly, "Mr. Elives, I need to talk to you."

"Go away!"

"But I need your help."

"Go away. I've helped you enough!"

"But I don't have any clothes."

"That's hardly my fault."

"But how can I get home?"

"Walk!"

"I can't do that!"

"Young man, if you do not leave my shop soon, I will show you a blast of magic that will make that silly ring I sold you seem like the toy it was. Now go!"

Russell stepped away from the curtains.

He was naked. How could he go home?

On the other hand, how could he stay here?

He thought it over. Considering how much trouble he was in already, being naked when he got home wasn't going to make that much difference.

But when he reached the door, he couldn't force himself to open it. The idea that had almost made sense thirty seconds ago now seemed insane.

He tried to convince himself.

It was Sunday morning. It was only about six o'clock, and the light was still dim. Hardly anyone would be up at this hour.

Besides, the bare fact was, there was nothing else he *could* do. He *had* to make a run for it.

At last his hand obeyed his orders.

He reached out, opened the door, and slipped through.

Immediately, he felt that everyone in the town was looking at him. Even the buildings seemed to have eyes.

Yet the world was strangely silent.

He shivered at the feel of the cool October air against his bare skin. Then he began to run.

When he reached the corner he noticed that the ring was gone. It must have slipped off when his hand had returned to normal. He hesitated for a moment. Did he want it back, or not?

He turned back toward the shop.

No. Gone was gone. The ring had caused him enough trouble already.

To his shock, he realized the shop was gone, too.

He decided maybe that wasn't so surprising after all.

Well...good-bye, ring, and good-bye, Mr. Elives. He waved a hand in farewell, then started to run.

Once the first fright had passed, Russell actually began to enjoy his homeward run. The chill in the air—and the sheer craziness of racing across town in his birthday suit—made him wildly alert. He felt open to the world, delighted by every sight and sound his greedy senses could absorb.

By taking to the backyards, he managed to remain unseen until he reached the development where he lived. Then, scooting behind a gray house, he saw a tired-looking woman standing at a window, holding a cup of coffee and gazing out with her eyelids at half-mast.

When she saw Russell, it looked as if someone had plugged in her curlers. Her eyelids shot up, her jaw dropped down, and coffee flew in all directions.

She strained to see who it was. But he was gone, trying not to let his laughter slow him down.

Five minutes later, he was home, and facing a new problem: What was the best way to get into the house? When he was a beast it had been easy, at least until he grew those wings. He would just scramble up the side of the house and through a window.

No way to do that now.

In fact, the only way in was through the front door, using the key hidden under the mat. Taking a deep breath, Russell scooted around to the front of the house. As he bent over to get the key he heard a scream from across the street.

It was Mrs. Micklemeyer. She had stepped out to get her morning paper. Now she stood with her hands pressed to her cheeks and her eyes bulging out.

Russell unlocked the door and slipped inside as fast as he could.

Peeking through the window, he saw Mrs. Micklemeyer staring at the house. Her face was twitching, as if she wasn't sure whether she should be showing anger or astonishment.

Well, that put an end to the idea that he could

keep his parents from knowing he had been running around without any clothes on. Mrs. Micklemeyer never kept her mouth shut. Actually, if she stayed true to form, the entire neighborhood would know he had been running around stark naked.

Shaking his head, he tiptoed up the stairway and toward his room. He opened the door, then stepped back quickly.

His mother was sitting in the chair beside his bed, sound asleep.

Russell was sure she had been there all night, waiting for him to come home.

He scurried down the hall to the bathroom, grabbed a towel, and wrapped it around his waist. Once back in his room, he switched it for his bathrobe, which hung on the bedpost. Then he went to his mother and gently shook her shoulder.

"Mom," he whispered. "I'm home!"

Her eyes flew open. She jumped up and threw her arms around him, hugging him close.

Hugging her back, he could feel her tears on his head.

"Where have you been?" she demanded, thrusting him away from her. Then she caught herself and pulled him close again. "Never mind," she said. "I'm just glad you're home."

Russell knew he would have to tell her something eventually. But for now, the words "Never mind"— words he didn't think he had ever heard her speak before—were just about the sweetest sound he had ever heard.

Epilogue

Russell was sitting in his room, thinking. Actually, he was supposed to be doing his homework. But thoughts of the ring kept pushing into his mind.

He wasn't sure why. He hadn't thought about it too much once everything had settled down after Halloween week. Of course, there had been a *lot* to settle down.

First he'd had to deal with his parents. He smiled as he remembered the story he had spun out to explain his absence that night.

Actually, the yarn had had bits of truth in it. He had blamed the trouble on the teenage boys, telling his parents that the boys had taken him into the woods and burned his clothes as a Halloween prank. His father had been furious and had wanted to call the police, but Russell had convinced him that there was no point in that, since the boys had been wearing masks and he had no idea who they were.

Then there had been Mr. Rafschnitz and his

wall-shaking lecture to Russell on the Monday after Halloween. (Not to mention two weeks of staying after school to pay for his crimes.)

And, of course, there was Eddie. His reaction to Russell in school after Halloween had been so comical that teachers and kids alike had besieged Russell with questions about what had happened. His noncommittal answers had not satisfied them but had left Eddie with some self-respect. Eddie seemed grateful for that.

All because of the ring.

Russell looked at the faint scar it had left on his finger and smiled.

Suddenly he felt a sharp pain just under the scar. He looked again, more closely.

The scar, usually almost invisible, was bright red.

And it was throbbing as if it were on fire.

What was going on?

Russell looked up and saw moonlight spilling over his windowsill—the light of the first full moon since Halloween.

His skin began to itch.

His forehead started to throb.

A wild urge to howl rose within him.

Now, finally, he understood what Mr. Elives had meant by "aftereffects."

He sighed.

"Well, Crannaker," he told himself, "that's what you get for not following directions."

Crossing to the window, he laid one hairy paw on the sill.

It was time to go out for the night.

A Note from the Author

It is probably no surprise to anyone who knows my books that Halloween is my favorite holiday. When I was a kid, I would haunt (you should pardon the expression) the library shelves during October, looking for just the right book to read on Halloween night. For me, the "right" book didn't just mean one that was scary. It meant one that had a combination of fright and fun, horror and humor—and, even more important, a sense of mystery and magic.

Though I found a lot of great books, I never did find just the one I was looking for. One reason I started writing *The Monster's Ring* was to fill that gap on the shelves, to come up with the perfect book to read on Halloween night.

Well, the book is not perfect, of course—which is all right with me, because that means I get to try again. Even so, it does contain most of the elements that I was looking for in a Halloween story.

One of those elements is Mr. Elives' magic shop,

which made its first appearance in this book. Basically, it's the magic shop I used to fantasize about finding when I was a kid myself. Even so, when I first wrote the book, I had no idea that I would come back to the shop so many times. But it is too interesting a place for me to stay away from—partly because I never know what's going to happen when I go back through its doors.

As the world of the shop has grown in my imagination, I have tried to weave more continuing elements through the books. That's why it was a pleasure to have a chance to revise this first book in the series.

I had to walk a delicate line in doing this work. I know that one of the things people have appreciated about *The Monster's Ring* is that it is compact, a book that parents have told me time and again is the first book their son or daughter ever read by themselves. I love hearing that, and I wanted to keep that lean, fast-paced quality.

But I also wanted to bring this edition of the book closer to the tone and style of the subsequent magic shop tales. In that regard, it was especially fun to weave in Roxanne and Jerome, the talking rats first introduced in *Jennifer Murdley's Toad*.

Oddly enough, a great deal of this book is based on real life. Russell and Eddie are both modeled on kids who were in my classes when I taught elementary school. Boardman Road Elementary itself is modeled on the school where I worked, though *our* principal was much nicer than "Beast" Rafschnitz. The geography of the school and its Halloween customs are taken from life. As, believe it or not, is the scene where Russell goes berserk at the Halloween party: It's drawn from the things that happened when my "half-mad twin brother, Igor" used to come for his annual Halloween visit. (I'll let you figure out the details on that one yourself.)

For me, the world of the magic shop is a place to celebrate mystery and marvels, a place where I go to remember that there is more wonder and strangeness swirling around us than we can ever understand.

A final note: I'm often asked for the correct pronunciation of the name of the man who runs the magic shop. The answer is easy. Just remember that "Mystery lives!"

The Magic Shop Books

THE BESTSELLING CLASSIC SERIES

Step inside Mr. Elives' magic shop—a place where boys hatch dragons, toads talk, rats deliver messages, and skulls spout Shakespeare. You are sure to find enchantment, adventure, insight, and fun!

"Will bring laughter and near tears to readers . . . Coville offers a fantasy that younger readers can handle easily, and one in which dragons really exist for a little while."   —*School Library Journal*

"Endlessly funny . . . A roller-coaster ride of a story, full of humor and even wisdom."
     —*Kirkus Reviews*

"A fast-moving, rollicking, yet serious tale . . . Will keep youngsters thinking. "
     —*School Library Journal*

"Although humorous, the story has surprising depth, with musings on honor, power, strength, courage, and, above all, love."   —*School Library Journal*